Nathaniel McDaniel AND THE Magic Attic

Bigbeard's Hook

BY Evan Solomon

ILLUSTRATED BY Bill Slavin

VIKING
CANADA

Acknowledgments

Nate goes nowhere without the magical help of Barbara Berson and her family;
the genius of Bill Slavin, Tracy Bordian, Debby de Groot, Mary Opper, Michael Levine,
and Maxine Quigley; the pirates Zoe and Jeremie; and the gang of four: Eden, Emmett,
Wyatt, and Maya. The Solomon and Quinn clans always bring their own magic, too,
as do folks at D Code. But dig deep enough and Nate will tell you that no story begins
without the love and support of Tammy, Maizie, and our new arrival, Gideon.

VIKING CANADA
Published by the Penguin Group

Penguin Group (Canada), 10 Alcorn Avenue, Toronto, Ontario, Canada M4V 3B2
 (a division of Pearson Penguin Canada Inc.)

Penguin Group (USA) Inc., 375 Hudson Street, New York, New York 10014, U.S.A.
Penguin Books Ltd, 80 Strand, London WC2R 0RL, England
Penguin Ireland, 25 St Stephen's Green, Dublin 2, Ireland (a division of Penguin Books Ltd)
Penguin Group (Australia), 250 Camberwell Road, Camberwell, Victoria 3124, Australia
 (a division of Pearson Australia Group Pty Ltd)
Penguin Books India Pvt Ltd, 11 Community Centre, Panchsheel Park, New Delhi – 110 017, India
Penguin Group (NZ), Cnr Airborne and Rosedale Roads, Albany, Auckland, New Zealand
 (a division of Pearson New Zealand Ltd)
Penguin Books (South Africa) (Pty) Ltd, 24 Sturdee Avenue, Rosebank, Johannesburg 2196,
 South Africa

Penguin Books Ltd, Registered Offices: 80 Strand, London WC2R 0RL, England

First published 2005   1 2 3 4 5 6 7 8 9 10 (GC)

Text copyright © Evan Solomon, 2005   Illustrations copyright © Bill Slavin, 2005
Hardcover ISBN 0-670-06386-X   Paperback ISBN 0-14-331215-4

Manufactured in Asia.

Library and Archives Canada Cataloguing in Publication data available upon request.

Visit the Penguin Group (Canada) website at **www.penguin.ca**

For Maizie, who opened our magic door
and took us on the greatest adventure of all
— E.S.

For Dawson, who is always the first to share my adventures
— B.S.

Nathaniel McDaniel loves to explore. He peeks into dressers and opens closed doors. He digs through closets and sifts through junk, and puts on old clothes that he finds in a trunk.

His big eyes are green, his shoes need repair,
and he *never* combs his straw-coloured hair.

When Sunday comes 'round …

... Nate visits his Gramps ...

... who lives in a mansion
and collects old stamps.

It's a grand place to dig, to hunt, hide, and seek.
Every nook and cranny is completely unique.

Nate stays the whole day until half-past six,
when Gramps grabs for his case
beside the gold candlesticks.
Then reaching inside,
Gramps makes a selection
and gives Nate a stamp
straight from his collection.

Nate shivers and smiles.
He goes red in his cheeks.
With a hug for his Gramps,
he'll be back next week.

One Sunday Nate spies
a hatch with a padlock.
He grins and he gawps,
"That must be the attic!"

But why such a lock …
and where is the key?
Nathaniel McDaniel
has so much to see.

The attic is secret,
his Gramps' special place.
No one else has been there,
left even a trace.

Nathaniel McDaniel begins to get sore.
With such a big lock,
how can he explore?

So … he picks it, he pokes it,
he practically chokes it.
He pulls it, he bangs it,
he even *harangues* it.

The lock holds firm,
refusing to budge, and
Nathaniel McDaniel develops a grudge.

"I'll smash down the hatch
then repair it with glue.
I'm exploring that attic
if it's the last thing I do!"

With one mighty heave
he bangs on the door,
then something falls

CLANG

hitting the floor.
The hatch hasn't moved,
that's easy to see, but
two feet away, there it is:
the KEY.

What luck!
What fortune!
Nate feels a chill.
The key has been hidden
on top of the sill.

With his small hands shaking,
he lets the lock slide.

One *click*,
  one *clack*,
    and he's on …

N ow, Nate's been in dressers
—oh, he's been in drawers—
but what he sees now makes
him sweat from his pores.

For inside the attic is like
nothing he's seen: artifacts,
treasures—an explorer's dream!

He sees ships in bottles
and old suits of armour.
Spices, devices, and a
wooden snake charmer.

There are dusty maps in
books and pirate hooks,
coins in great tins and
giant mammoth skins.

Swords and masks
and dry gunpowder.
Paintings and bones and
jars of clam chowder.

Tiger teeth, moon rocks,
a ventriloquist's dummy,
a lantern, a compass,
and an Egyptian mummy.

Nate leaps in the air. He dances and twirls.
He's just found the very best room in the world!
What to touch first: a bone, bat, or book? *But …*
he's drawn to a terrifying old pirate's hook.
It's deadly and sharp, and covered in dust.
There's blood on its point—or could it be rust?

Tiptoeing slowly, Nate chews his thumbnail
(he always feels tingly on the explorer's trail).
Reaching out his hand,
he grabs hold of the rarity,

when …

BA-ZANG

there's a cosmic irregularity.

As soon as Nate clutches that cold piece of metal,
the room starts to boil all hot like a kettle.
He sways and he stumbles. His stomach feels fizzy.
Nathaniel McDaniel begins to get dizzy.
With eyes shut tight he hears a great *Rrrip!*

and suddenly

he's on board …

I t's an old Spanish galleon, not much more than a wreck,
with pirates all 'round him swabbing the deck.
Just what's happened he hasn't a notion.
How did he get here, on the Atlantic Ocean?

"Avast, wee sailor!" cries a man with a sword.
"Get to work or I'll throw ye overboard."

Nathaniel McDaniel gulps and he stares.
For the first time in years he feels kinda scared.
But he raises his fists and shouts, "You'd better stay away!"
Then the man hisses, "Mates, we gots us a stowaway."

He yanks Nate up close,
his breath fishy and rank.
"How's it gonna feel, boy,
to be walkin' the plank?"

The pirates all cheer. They snarl and they bark,
"Feed the wee lad to the great white shark!"
Then a splash and a blast from the ocean beneath:

out leaps a shark …

with twelve rows of teeth.

Nate squirms and he fights to save his young life
as each man in the mob pulls out a knife.
Then just as Nathaniel gives up his resistance,
he spots something moving off in the distance.
"Navy ship approaching, sailing due west!"
comes a bellow from way up in the crow's nest.
The pirates all scatter to the lee cannon side

and Nathaniel knows ...

this is the best time to hide.

He slips below deck and heads straight for the stern.
With so much confusion, which way should he turn?
Behind him he hears, "There goes the wee lad!"
So Nate starts to run like an Olympiad.
As he bursts through a door to escape the buccaneers,
a voice *growls* ...

Nathaniel goes pale when he spies a cocked pistol,
for the man in the room is the terror of Bristol.
Nate's seen pictures of that one-eyed blue stare
and the great chin that sprouts ten feet of red hair.

"Who are ye?" asks Bigbeard, swilling some rye.
"Ye better start talkin' if ye don't want to die."

Nathaniel McDaniel doesn't know
what to say, so he gets on his knees
and he starts to pray. But Bigbeard
doesn't shoot (and this is no lie);
instead he wells up with tears
in his one great eye.

"I ain't gonna harm ye,"
Bigbeard chokes back a sob.
"For a pirate with no hook
is like a man with no job."

Nate's confused for a moment but soon
understands: the great Captain Bigbeard
is missing his hand!
Now Nathaniel is clever, as everyone knows,
and he's hidden the hook deep inside of
his clothes. If he plays this out right
and isn't too hasty, that hook is his ticket
back home to safety.

"What happened to your talon?" Nate asks, all nervous.
"If I can help in any way, I'm at your service."

"We was boardin' a French vessel," Bigbeard whimpers, then coughs,
"when some rascal, he jumped me and pulled it right off.
With a flourish and dash—that's the French specialty—
that wretch tossed me claw right into the sea.
Oh, what I'd do to have me hook back once more.
I'd give all that I have in me treasure store."

With that Nate marches forward, crying, "Looky right here!"
and he hangs that hook from Bigbeard's bandolier.
The pirate erupts. He roars and he rears.
He's so excited he trips on his beard.
"Me hook! Ye found it? Egads and blimey!"
Then Bigbeard frowns and his face turns
mean …

dark …

and slimy.

"I guess ye'll be wantin' to collect yer reward.
    Well, Sonny, here she be!" and he pulls out his sword.
  "I don't know where ye got it—that's not my concern—'cause
    crossing Bigbeard's the last lesson ye'll learn."

    He advances toward Nathaniel then, that
villainous crook, starts to reattach his beloved hook.
      "I'd like to thank ye, boy, for returning me joint.
  Now let me show ye what I likes to do with its point."

But the moment the hook clicks onto Bigbeard's
stump, the ship starts to shudder, to quake, and to jump.

Nate sways and he stumbles. His stomach feels fizzy.
All of a sudden he begins to get dizzy. The last thing
Nate sees is the pirate's swordplay when

there's that feeling that takes him away.
He shuts his eyes tight and hears some loud static,

and next thing

he knows...

... he's back in the attic.

Nate's made his escape—it was pretty near tragic.
Still, he's discovered a room
full of stuff that is magic.
'Cause whatever he touches
takes him through time and through space,
until the artifact is returned
to its proper place.

Nathaniel McDaniel wants to stay there and roam,
but it's close to six-thirty and he has to get home.

So he steps through the hatch and closes the lock,
puts the key in his pocket and swears not to talk.

As Nate creeps down the stairs he sees his folks waiting.
"What's the matter?" asks Dad. "You're hesitating?"
Gramps gives Nate a wink and gets off his chair.
"Come here," he whispers. "I'll give you something quite rare."
Gramps opens his case and makes a selection.
He gives Nate a stamp
straight from his collection.

Nathaniel bends down to take a closer look,
and there's old Bigbeard holding his hook.
What a fluke! What a chance! It's truly a mystery.
"Hey, Nate," chuckles Gramps, "don't you love history?"

Nathaniel shivers and smiles. He goes red in his cheeks.

With a hug for his Gramps …

... he'll be back
next week.

Watch for Nate's
next adventure in
The Sabre-Toothed Tiger